KT-157-030

Wanda the Witch's Party

You have been invited to a party in my house. I am busy getting ready, so go ahead (enter my front door) and find your own way (by following the paths and going up and down the stairs, steps, ladders and slides) through my house to the party (at the back of the book)!

If you come to a deadend (a room with no way out), turn back and find a different path. But remember, be careful which route you take - Warto the wicked wizard might be lurking behind the door, ready to cast a spell on you (send you back several pages).

Have fun and remember to pick up the key that you will find in one of the rooms. You will need it in order to enter the party once you get there!

Good Luck!

Wanda

Published by Lagoon Books
PO Box 311, KT2 5QW, UK
PO Box 990676, Boston, MA 02199, USA

ISBN: 1902813111
© Lagoon Books, 2000. Lagoon Books is a trademark of Lagoon Trading Company Ltd. All rights reserved.

1
WELCOME

2

3
SPELLS

4

5

PLANS
OIL
OIL

JET
YOU CANNOT ENTER THIS ROOM WITHOUT FINDING MY BROOM

GO BACK TO THE START OF PAGE 2
GO FORWARD TO THE LANDING ON PAGE 10, WHERE THE PIRATES ARE HAVING A SWORD FIGHT

GO BACK TO THE ROOM WITH THE GIANT TOAD IN IT ON PAGE 5

GO BACK TO THE TOP LANDING ON PAGE 3, WHERE THE WIZARD IS READING HIS SPELL BOOK

GO BACK TO THE ROOM WITH THE HOT AIR BALLOON IN IT ON PAGE 7

flour
flour

TO WANDA
GO BACK TO THE VAT OF CHOCOLATE ON PAGE 8

ENTER NOT UNLESS
YOU'VE FOUND A
PRESENT FOR WANDA

GO BACK TO THE BUBBLING CAULDRON AT THE TOP OF PAGE 4
TRAVEL UP THESE STAIRS ONLY. YOU CANNOT COME DOWN
INK

20
GO BACK TO THE PIRATE SHIP ON PAGE 11
WANDA'S PARTY
DID YOU BRING ME THE KEY? IF SO, COME IN. IF NOT, GO BACK AND FIND IT!
WELL DONE AND WELCOME TO MY PARTY!
WANDA